LITTLE GIRLS
LOST

~ By ~

Vickie L. Kreeger

PublishAmerica
Baltimore

First printing

ISBN: 1-60563-229-5
PUBLISHED BY PUBLISHAMERICA, LLLP
www.publishamerica.com
Baltimore

Printed in the United States of America

This book is dedicated to my wonderful husband, Rick for all of the encouragement, love, and support he has given me throughout not only this endeavor, but everything in life.

CHAPTER ONE

Lily Fernstat smiled and waved to the mailman as she reached for the bundle of envelopes in his outstretched hand. She thumbed through the pile as she made her way back up the long driveway of the farm that had been in her family for more than a hundred years. Seeing nothing but the ordinary bills and advertisements, she let her eyes wander and enjoyed her walk back to the house.

The Fernstat farm was a typical Midwestern farm lying just outside of the small town of Bridgewater Falls. The large white two-story clapboard farm house with its sprawling front porch was situated to the right of the driveway and showed its age only through the majestic century old Burr Oak trees dotting the front lawn.

The only exception to typical was the aged, but neatly kept mobile home the color of an avocado with a set of steps leading up to the door standing to the left of the driveway. Flower beds filled with multi colored petunias, pansies, and snap dragons lined both sides of the steps in an attempt to beautify the outside.

Beyond the trailer and farm house, an old red barn stood tall and proud with lines of white fencing surrounding it and the nearby pasture. The perimeters of the property stretched a mile in all directions with the same white fencing enclosing the sprawling fields, orchards, and creek.

Lily smiled to herself as she glimpsed her two granddaughters playing under a willow tree outside of the trailer. She remembered the day her daughter, Laurel, had approached her about moving into the trailer with Jenna, who was just a baby at the time.

Lily agreed immediately, elated with the opportunity to spend more time with the precious little baby she so dearly loved. Not to mention how nice it would be to have her daughter once again living on the farm with her. Lily's son, Chase, had remained on the farm after his father's death to take over the main operations, but Laurel had married and moved into town with her husband. A year and a half later, Laurel filed for divorce and became increasingly more afraid of her estranged husband, Matthew. Sighing contentedly, Lily waved to the girls before opening the door to the kitchen of the farm house and disappearing inside.

Rubbing her sore eyes, Laurel Monroe yawned as she scuffed her stockinged feet through the hall from her bedroom, "Coffee, I need coffee," she drawled sleepily.

WHAP! "Ooooouuuuuccchhhh!" she cried as she stubbed her toe. Grabbing her throbbing foot, she hopped in pain as she looked around the living room.

Frustrated, Laurel, hands on hips, eyed the pile of toys scattered about her feet. The longer she stood in the midst of it, with her pulsating toe, the angrier she became, she was already exhausted from the lack of sleep and to wake up to this. This had to stop, Jenna knew better than to leave a mess like this and she was going to put an end to it once and for all.

"Jennnna, get your butt in here and pick up this mess," Laurel yelled from the door of the trailer.

"Noooo, mommy, can't I do it later? Laci and I wanna play."

"Jenna Marie, get your butt in here, NOW, or I'm getting the belt."

Still refusing, five-year old Jenna called her mother's bluff. Flying from the trailer, Laurel grabbed her by the seat of the pants, mind set on teaching her daughter the consequences of disobeying.

Jenna's feet never touched the ground as she was tossed into the mound of books and puzzles on the living room floor.

"Now start picking up," Laurel huffed leaving the room.

Tears falling, Jenna stacked the books and puzzles she and little three-year old Laci had played with. Stifling a sob she turned as she heard her mother come into the room, dangling from her hand was the belt.

Releasing a sob, Jenna turned to finish picking up. She didn't know why she pushed her mom to the limits because she knew what would happen.

"Stand up and come over here." Rising slowly to postpone the inevitable, Jenna, head down, tears streaming, approached.

"Now turn around." Jenna did as she was told and leaned over her mother's knee.

Later that evening, Laurel crossed the driveway and wearily climbed the porch steps of the old farm house. She held the screen door as her mother carried a tray of lemonade to a small table on the porch. Laurel took a seat in one of the two wicker rockers as Lily poured them each a glass.

Lily took her seat in the remaining chair. "Ahhh, this is my favorite part of the day. Dinner is over, the dishes are done and there's nothing left to do but relax and enjoy what's left of the evening."

Laurel remained silent as she tucked her feet under her and laid her head against the back of the chair, watching the girls play in the yard.

Lily studied her daughters somber expression. "You're awfully quiet tonight." Lately she noticed bags under Laurel's eyes and a paleness to her skin and worried for her health.

"Mmmm, I'm tired, that's all," she replied as she sipped her lemonade.

"Matthew again?"

Laurel dropped her head and focused on her hands, fighting back tears, she nodded. "Isn't it always?" Sniffling, she wiped her eyes with the back of her hand. "I don't know what he wants from me." Lily remained silent as she rocked giving the opportunity for Laurel to continue.

"I mean, night after night, he's outside my door," sitting forward she cried, "and if I have to listen to that stupid doorknob rattle much longer I'm gonna go crazy."

Stopping the rocker, Lily reached for her glass. "What do you think he wants?"

Frustrated, Laurel went on, "I think he's losing his mind, I really believe he thinks we're still married. I'm so terrified at night because I don't know what he'd do if he got in."

Lily looked at the red streaks on her daughter's face with concern. "Why don't you get the police involved, honey?"

Laurel shot her mother a look of shock. "My god, mom, I can't do that, not with his temper. He'd kill me." She watched as the girls snuck up on an unsuspecting butterfly before adding, "and Jenna, doesn't help matters any. She's always getting in to things and making me so angry, I..."

"LAUREL, I know you're tired and under a lot of stress, but you can't take that out on the girls. Jenna already has one parent who resents her, she doesn't need another. She's five years old, Laurel, of course she's going to get in to things, that's what kids do."

Tears fell down Laurel's face. "I know and I always feel so bad afterwards," clearing the sob from her throat she continued, "but it's so hard raising them alone. There's no way I can let him take them anywhere because he may never bring them back. I'd die if that happened, they're my kids and they need me,"

Wiping her tears she smiled as the two of them giggled and squealed when the butterfly they were pursuing flew away.

"Dear, you really need to figure this out, because you can't go on like this," Lily commented with concern.

"I know, I know," Laurel slapped her hands on her knees. "But right now I need to get a couple of little girls into the tub and into bed."

Lily knew that was her daughters way of telling her the conversation was over, so she let it go. "It's supposed to storm tonight."

Looking at the ominous clouds overhead, Laurel stood. "Come on girls, time for bed." After bidding her mother good night she headed for the trailer with Jenna and Laci close behind.

Lightning flashed as Laurel pulled the covers back and climbed in next to a sleeping Jenna. She was more comfortable since moving the girls into her bedroom several months ago. Thunder clapped nearby causing her to draw the covers closer under her chin as she lay wide-eyed in the darkness.

The dark nights were terrifying and the thunderstorm was creating havoc on her already rattled nerves. On nights such as this, her senses enhanced every flash, every noise, tenfold, and every tree branch took on the ominous form of knife-wielding maniacs in the flashes of light.

Laurel spent many nights lying awake knowing Matthew was out there—waiting. She could hear his footsteps climbing the steps. He was out there and she was frightened.

She quietly rose from the bed and looked down on Jenna's sleeping face, crossing the room to the crib she checked Laci. Sleeping. Shifting her eyes nervously between the sleeping girls and the bedroom door, Laurel's heart furiously pounded as she moved toward the opening. She hated when her fear became so overwhelming she second guessed herself locking the front door. The same scene had played out night after night since her divorce, frightening her so badly she couldn't remember if she had locked it or not.

Laurel closed her eyes and took a deep breath in an attempt at calming her fear. Lightning continued flashing shadows through the darkness as she crept silently through the hall. Approaching the window, she peeked through a crack in the curtain and scanned the trees, he could be anywhere out there—hiding, tormenting.

She let the curtain drop as she spotted a figure cloaked in darkness running through the yard, inhaling sharply she flattened her body against the wall. She had to get to the door before he did, being careful to stay out of the light, she ducked under the window and darted for the door.

Laurel lifted her hand to check the lock, the doorknob rattled. Too late. Please let the door be locked. The sweat beaded on her forehead and her pulse raced wildly as she quickly slid her back against the wall. This was it. He was coming in.

She put her fingers around the heavy doorstop and lifted it above her head—waiting. After what felt like a lifetime the rattling stopped and the footsteps retreated, but Laurel remained quietly sitting with the doorstop gripped tightly in her hands as she had so many nights before.

CHAPTER TWO

It wasn't Matthew Monroe's nature to be a doting father. It wasn't his nature to be any kind of father for that matter, to his daughters he was merely a man known as Matthew, whom they seldom saw and had never called daddy.

Famous for avoiding Laci all together, Laurel wasn't surprised when Matthew showed up during her nap, but bless her heart, Jenna was excited to see him every time he came through the door. Shifting his weight, he squatted once he realized Laurel wasn't going to offer him a chair.

Intentionally ignoring Jenna's attempts at getting his attention, Matthew turned to his ex-wife. "How's it going?"

"Good." Clenching her teeth as she seethed with anger. Laurel didn't understand why it would kill him to show the little girl some affection, but knew it wasn't anything new.

"Matthew, Matthew, I rode my pony yesterday." Excitedly Jenna jumped up and down.

Continuing his conversation without a glance in his daughter's direction. "Did you get my last check?"

Jenna grasped his face in her hands turning it to look at her. "I started kindergarten…."

Forcing his head out of her hands with a disgusted jerk, he looked once again at her mother as she replied, "Yeah, I got it."

Desperate to get his attention, Jenna grabbed his keys, jiggling them and dancing, "Nah, nah, na, nah, nah." Her efforts went unnoticed, dejectedly she sighed and noticed a knife hanging on the keychain. Turning it over and over in her hand.....

"Let go of that knife," Matthew screamed as he gripped her arm and put her over his knee. The first few strikes on her backside hurt like the dickens, not only from the lashing itself, but from humiliation and rejection. After several whacks on the behind, he gripped her roughly by the arms. "You better straighten up and start minding, young lady."

Devastated, Jenna ran out the door and across the yard to her grandma's house. Sobbing, she opened the door and ran into the open arms of her grandmother. Lily hugged the sweet child before sitting down and settling her on her lap.

Laurel's heart sank as she watched her daughter run out the door. "What's wrong with you? She sees you once every few months and you do this."

Matthew rose to his feet and took a sauntering step toward her with his eyes fixed on hers. "I don't come here to see her," commenting as he took another step.

Fear rose in Laurel's throat as she stepped backward. "Matthew, Stop." The look in his eyes gave her an unsettling feeling. "Don't come any closer or I'll..."

Another step. "Or you'll what, Laurel," throwing his hands toward her, "Call the cops?" He took another step forward as he laid his head back and laughed.

Backing her into the corner, a tear slipped from the corner of her eye as she pleaded, "Please, please Matthew."

She watched his hand move to the button of his jeans as he stepped closer. "There is only one reason I come over here and it isn't to see them two brats of yours."

Laurel turned her head away and released a small whimper as he pressed his body against her. "Please don't," she begged as he ran his tongue up her neck. Laurel let out a sob as she heard his zipper and felt his hardness press against her belly.

"You know what I want, Laurel," he whispered against her throat.

"No, please."

"God, I love it when you beg." She whimpered again as he undid her pants, "And just in case you get it in your head to scream..." He placed the blade of his pocket knife under her chin, he worked her pants down and entered her.

"This is the way it was meant to be Laurel, you loved it then and you love it now. It could have always been this way." As he rammed her against the wall. "But, no, you had to go and get yourself pregnant." Another thrust and he smiled. "You're mine, Laurel, you'll always be mine."

He grabbed a handful of her hair as he circled her breast with the blade of his knife. "Don't ever deny me what's mine, bitch," he spit in her face as he thrust hard against her driving his point home, "or you may just find your precious brats..."

Laurel sobbed as he found his release and with a menacing grin, stepped away from her trembling body and zipped his pants.

Just as Laurel finished buttoning her jeans, the front door flew open and Jenna came running in still sniffling. "Matthew, your wife just called and said for you to get home, NOW!"

"She did not."

"Yes she did and gramma said she's real mad."

"No she didn't," Matthew replied no longer sure what to believe.

"Okay, don't listen, but gramma said you're gonna be in big trouble when you get home."

Laurel took this as her cue. "I think you need to leave now, Laci's about ready to get up from her nap." Searching her eyes, he reluctantly nodded and left without a word.

Laurel closed the door behind him, resting her forehead against it. She knew she would pay for that tonight.

Pulling on her mother's shirt. "Mommy, what's the matter?"

Forcing a smile to her face, Laurel turned to her daughter. "Nothing, sweetheart, nothing at all. How about we go wake up your sister, huh?" Jenna nodded and ran down the hallway to the bedroom intent on waking Laci and no sooner had the two of them come out of the bedroom, they were outside exploring.

Laurel sat on the sofa with her chin resting on the back of her hand as she watched them play out the window. She smiled as she watched Jenna put a finger to her lips. "Shhh, Laci be real quiet." The girls tiptoed their way to a big wooden electrical box.

Pausing in front of it, Jenna put her hand on the door and quickly threw it open. Laurel laughed with tears in her eyes as she watched the two of them scream and run away as the little mice they surprised ran wildly for cover.

She let the tears fall freely as she remembered her life with Matthew. Things had been wonderful between them, they loved, they laughed, and they loved some more. That was until Laurel became pregnant with Jenna.

Laurel was ecstatic about the news and couldn't wait for Matthew to get home to tell him. They never really discussed children before, but he loved her so much, she knew he'd be thrilled. She planned a special meal with candlelight, wine, and soft music to share the news with him.

"What's the special occasion?" he asked as he took her in his arms and felt the familiar passions stir to life. Laurel put her arms around his neck as she leaned her head back, allowing him to spray her neck with light kisses.

"I've got something to tell you," she replied breathlessly as his lips teased her ear. They had been married for little over a year and still enjoyed a very passionate marriage.

Nuzzling the area between her breasts he murmured, "Hmmm, what's that?"

Enjoying his caress, she whispered, "I had an appointment today."

Moving his hand to his wife's beautiful bosoms straining at the top of her blouse, he murmured, "Hmmmm."

Laying her head back to allow him full access. "I'm pregnant." Cold water couldn't have had more of an effect on Matthew. His hands stopped as he snapped his head. "WHAT?"

Confused. "I, I, I thought you would be happy. Matthew, I know it's a shock, but you're going to be a daddy."

Pushing her away from him, he headed for the door. "Get rid of it." He walked out and slammed the door behind him, leaving Laurel surrounded by candlelight—alone.

Snapping back to reality, Laurel swiped the tears from her cheeks as she stood and headed for the kitchen. She added a squirt of dish soap as she filled the sink with soapy water and set to washing dishes….

That was the beginning of the end to her perfect marriage. Matthew stayed away for several days after that night. Laurel's news caused something in him to snap and he was never the same loving Matthew she had married.

When he did return, his reactions were as if the incident hadn't happened, but not as if he were pretending it didn't happen, that she could have dealt with. His behavior was that everything was the same as the day before the incident, although with a coldness about him.

Matthew's strange behavior began to frighten Laurel. He no longer looked at her with the deep seated love he once had, but instead with an empty robotically coldness about him.

For months he took her in his arms and cried against her hair, "I don't know what I would do if anything happened to you." Not getting a response, he pushed her to arms length and glared into her eyes. "There's someone else isn't there? ISN'T THERE?" he screamed, then realizing what he had done, pulled her close and whispered forebodingly, "I will never share you, Laurel, with anyone. Do you hear me, ANYONE."

His erratic behavior led to his playing cruel jokes on her as he sat sadistically by laughing at her reactions. Once he went as far as having his twin brother, Michael, pretend to be him and make love to her as he himself snuck quietly into the house to sit on the sofa, awaiting her entrance into the living room.

After Jenna was born, things grew worse until fearing for her child's safety, Laurel had enough and kicked him out. He stood outside of their house every night, yelling at her, "I TOLD YOU, LAUREL, I'LL NEVER SHARE YOU WITH ANYONE." Over and over he ranted.

Laurel laid on the living room floor protecting the baby's body with her own as he went on a rampage, pulling a gun and shooting at the house, "YOU BETTER LET ME IN, LAUREL, I'M YOUR HUSBAND AND I'M NOT GOING AWAY."

Screaming as a bullet hit the side of the house, Laurel gave way to the fear inside of her and sobbed, "Go away, leave me alone."

"YOU'RE MINE LAUREL, YOU'LL ALWAYS BE MINE. YOU CAN'T GO ANYWHERE I CAN'T FIND YOU." Staying low to the floor, Laurel reached for the phone and did what she knew she should have done a long time ago.

Laurel hugged the baby tightly to her as she watched the police subdue Matthew and force him into a straight jacket. Her brother protectively shielded her as Matthew was put onto a stretcher and taken away.

Matthew spent a month in the mental hospital, until Laurel could no longer deal with the harassment his family was giving her and signed him out. Upon Matthew's release, Laurel filed for divorce and was awarded full custody of Jenna. That was five years ago…

Bringing herself back to the present. "Shit," Laurel put her finger in her mouth and headed for the bathroom to get a Band-Aid, when she realized she had broken a glass and cut herself. "That's what happens when you don't keep your mind on what your doing," she told herself as she wiped the blood away and headed for the door to get the girls for dinner.

Laurel was right, he was back at the door later that night. Tears streamed down her cheeks as she gripped the doorstop once again waiting for him to come through the door. Once again, he didn't. She knew he was playing with her mind as he let go of the doorknob and retreated down the steps.

Laurel lowered the object in her hand and gave way to her pent up sobs wondering when his tormenting would end.

CHAPTER THREE

The terrifying ordeal of the previous night left Laurel physically and mentally drained. Laying Laci down for an early nap and shooing Jenna out to play, she settled herself in for some much needed rest.

Running down the steps, Jenna smiled catching sight of her uncle outside of the barn. "Hey, Uncle Chase, what are ya doing?" Her tawny pony tail bobbing as she skipped toward him.

"Hey, toad, I'm tryin to get this old tractor runnin'. I'm going out to the orchard to mend some fence." Chase flashed her a big smile as he filled the tank of the old international with gas. The tractor had definitely seen better days, but as long as it started it remained a part of the farm.

"Why don't you run into the barn and get me a hammer and a box of nails."

"Can I come, too," Jenna asked over her shoulder, running into the barn.

She found the hammer laying on a post of one of the stalls, she grabbed it along with a box of nails on the floor. Taking time to stop and pet the soft nose of her Shetland pony, she gave her a hand full of oats from the bucket. Picking up the hammer and nails she laid on the floor she said, "Bye Daisy," and bounced out of the barn as the pony gave a soft nicker.

Back outside, Uncle Chase had the tractor running and was waiting as he lifted her to sit in front of him. It was a beautiful day, the sun was bright, the sky a brilliant blue with soft billowing clouds as they took off on the rough trek to the orchard. Inhaling deeply the sweet scent of clover, Jenna bounced in her seat as they made their way through the pasture. She smiled as Chase pointed to a couple of deer running into the timber, probably to a baby or two hidden in the brush.

Chase stopped the tractor and hopped off. "Stay here, toad, and don't touch anything, I'll be right back." He disappeared into a thicket of trees and undergrowth.

Jenna looked around suddenly feeling alone. The orchard was eerily quiet with the exception of the putt-putting of the tractor.

Jenna asked softly, "Uncle Chase, are you there?" Uncomfortable being alone, she busied herself pretending she was driving the tractor on a high speed chase. Squealing tires as she turned corners and bouncing in her seat.

Accidentally she hit the brake release. "Uh oh, Uncle Chaaaassseee, ahhhhh," Jenna screamed as the tractor lurched forward. Holding on for dear life, hair blowing in the wind, Jenna plummeted down the hill past a stunned Uncle Chase.

Frantic, Chase ran after the runaway tractor. "Jenna, Jennnnnaaaaa, hold on," screaming as he ran.

Jenna screamed and bounced in the seat and headed for a tree, she saw it coming but her legs were too short to reach the brake and left her helpless to prevent the crash.

"Oh my God, Jenna are you all right?" Checking her for injuries and finding none he hugged her then firmly gripped her under the arms and deposited her not-so-gently on the ground.

"What were you thinking young lady, you could've been killed."

"I'm sorry Uncle Chase, but I was scared and you wouldn't answer me, I bumped something and the tractor started going and I couldn't reach the pedal." Nervously shifting his eyes to the thicket of trees he had just emerged from, Chase hopped up into the seat of the tractor, Jenna shook with fear, afraid he was leaving her alone in the orchard. He rocked the tractor back and forth until he worked it back up the hill.

Reaching down he grabbed Jenna and put her in front of him once again. "Listen, toad, I had to check a coon trap in the brush back there. Now if you promise not to tell your mom or gramma I left you alone on the tractor, I promise not to tell them you crashed. Deal?"

"Deal!" Jenna answered happy just to be safe on her uncle's lap.

Jenna held true to her promise and didn't tell anyone of their adventure in the orchard. Arriving home, Chase put the tractor in the barn as Laci ran down the driveway toward Jenna standing by the water trough. "Sissy, what you doing?"

"Looking at the goldfish, wanna see?" She asked her little sister.

"Uh huh." Laci nodded.

Jenna pulled on a cement block, catching her foot, she stumbled. Getting up and brushing herself off, she dragged it to the horse trough for Laci to stand on. Helping her little sister up they peered at the fish Uncle Chase kept in the tank during the summer.

They loved watching the fish swim gracefully around the tank. Laci put her fingers in the water and let the fish suck on them as she giggled, "That tickles, Sissy." For as long as Jenna could remember, Laci called her sissy.

"It does tickle," Jenna replied putting an arm around her little sister.

Chase came out of the barn. "Come on girls, let's go eat."

Giggling as he picked her up, Laci gave him a hug and Jenna took his hand as they crossed the yard to the house.

Several hours after tucking the girls into bed Laurel sat alone in the dark—waiting. The bags under her eyes had given way to an unsettling hollowness and her heart skipped a beat as the familiar sounds signaled the start to her nightly ritual. Trembling she turned a haunted look to the door as the sadistic rattling began. She knew somehow, someway tonight would be different and she braced herself for what was to come.

CHAPTER FOUR

Stretching and yawning, Laurel rolled on to her back. Rubbing the sleep from her eyes, she squinted as the bright morning sun fell across her face.

"Uhhh," she grunted plopping a pillow over her head. She didn't want to get up, the frightening late nights were taking a toll. Unable to go back to sleep, she felt Jenna's side of the bed. Empty.

Many mornings Jenna woke early and helped Laci out of the crib. Laurel was grateful on the days when Jenna fed her little sister cereal, allowing her to sleep in.

Throwing back the covers, Laurel sat up. "Girls, mommy's going to take a shower." She stumbled to the dresser and chose a pair of jean shorts and a tank top before heading to the bathroom.

Feeling refreshed, Laurel walked into the quiet living room. "Jenna. Laci. Girls,"

Receiving no answer. "Hmmm, they must have already gone outside." She started a pot of coffee and headed back to the bedroom to make beds. Finishing the bed, she picked up the girls discarded clothes and put them in the hamper.

Heading into the kitchen, Laurel poured herself a cup of the freshly brewed coffee and sat down at the table. Finishing her coffee, she rose placing her cup in the sink, noticing the lack of dirty cereal bowls, she headed for the door.

"Jenna, what were you thinking not getting your sister something to eat,"

The screen door slammed behind her as Laurel hustled down the steps and marched toward the barn. Once inside, she spotted her brother spreading fresh straw in the stalls.

"Have you seen Jenna and Laci this morning?"

"No, I can't say that I have, they're probably with mom up at the house," Chase suggested as he spread another fork full.

"You're probably right," Laurel said as she glanced around the barn. She couldn't shake the prickly feeling of apprehension creeping up her spine. "I'll go check." One more glance around the barn and she left.

The closer she drew to the house, the more her stomach knotted. Reaching for the screen door, she entered the kitchen to find her mother busy baking—alone.

"Where's the girls, mom?"

Wiping flour from her hands on her apron, she turned to Laurel. "I'm not sure, I haven't seen them yet this morning."

"Are you sure you haven't seen them?" Panic filled Laurel and her voice grew higher.

"They have to be here somewhere, they are probably just outside playing, don't get yourself all worked up in a tizzy until we've had a chance to look for them," Lily said as she removed her apron to help look for Jenna and Laci. "Let's get Chase and we'll start looking."

CHAPTER FIVE

As Lily and Laurel approached, Chase could tell from the look on their faces, the girls were not with his mother. "Don't worry, sis, we'll find them." Chase then turned his gaze to his mother. "Mom, you and Laurel check around here in the barns and any of their favorite play places. I'll saddle up and check the orchard."

"I better fix you some sandwiches," Lily threw over her shoulder, already on her way to the house.

She was surprised with the authoritative attitude her son had taken. Laurel liked to be center of attention, she thrived for it. She had learned long ago the more drama life threw in her twenty-six year old daughter's direction, the happier Laurel was. On the other hand, at twenty-three, Chase preferred to stay out of the limelight and remain subtly in the background.

Hugging herself as tears puddled in her eyes, Laurel walked to the door of the barn. Where could they be, she wondered as she surveyed the distant horizon.

Feeling a reassuring squeeze of her shoulder, she pressed her cheek against his hand. "We—will—find them, sis."

Swiping at the stray tear, Laurel looked up into the sapphire eyes of her brother. "I know, it's just that so many things are running through my mind right now and none of them are good."

With one last squeeze, he grabbed his saddle and headed out the door toward his horse. Lily walked up with the sandwiches and a thermos of coffee, just as her son was mounting up. After watching him ride off, they began the search of the grounds.

"Jennnnaaaaa. Laaaacccciiii," Laurel called as she frantically searched through the shed. At the door, she put a hand to her eyes blocking the sun as she spotted the big wooden electrical box beside the trailer and headed in that direction.

Reaching for and opening the door, she jumped as the little mice, Jenna and Laci loved to watch, ran off. Settling her nerves, Laurel closed the door and shook her head, wondering what the girls found so fascinating about the creepy little things.

Reining his horse to a stop, Chase studied his surroundings, he was at the place in the orchard, he and Jenna had their mishap.

Tearing his eyes from the thicket and talking to his horse, "I've been calling and searching for hours, maybe it's time to call the sheriff." Turning his horse around, he headed for home.

Chase entered the kitchen, laid his hat on the counter and headed for the sink to wash up. "It's gonna be dark soon," he remarked, gazing out the window as he wiped his hands on a towel before turning to Lily's grief-stricken face.

"Oh, Chase, they're too little to be out there alone," Lily choked.

Chase's eyes left his mothers and settled on the back of Laurel's head as she stood looking out the window. "I'm gonna give the sheriff a call." Picking up the receiver, Chase hesitated and took a deep breath before punching in the numbers 9-1-1.

CHAPTER SIX

The Fernstat farm was a flurry of activity as deputies and volunteer search teams arrived, quickly filling the yard with squad cars, trucks, and horse trailers. Volunteers and deputies alike were divided into search teams and awaiting instructions.

Inside the farm house, Sheriff Dan Thompson picked up a picture sitting on the fireplace mantle and studied it along with the many others nestled along the length of it. He looked down at the one in his hand where two little girls with tawny colored pigtails were smiling broadly as they wrapped their arms around their mother.

Taking a step back he took note of the interior of the house. The living room was very open and airy, yet homey with its huge stone fireplace covering an entire wall. An overstuffed couch sitting in front of the large picture window overlooking the front porch and yard was covered with a handmade quilt, Dan was certain must be a Fernstat family heirloom. Two mismatched end tables adorned each end of the couch and were also more than likely from early family members. The tables had delicate hand embroidered cloths draped over them and each held a lamp and several family photos.

The picture window was adorned with gold flowered curtains tied back on each side. There were a couple of worn recliners situated at one end of the room with another table between them and an old wooden rocker with a pillowed cushion.

The console television centered on the remaining wall looked as if it was on its last leg and held several figurines. The hardwood floor was visible around the edges of the large oval rag rug covering most of it. The beige colored walls sported several framed landscape paintings and the wall directly across from the front door had an archway in the center leading to the dining room and kitchen.

Holding his hat in his hand. "Uhhh, excuse me sheriff, the teams are ready."

Placing his hat on his head, Dan Thompson, turned to Laurel, who was sitting with her mother on the overstuffed couch. "We are going to find them, Mrs. Monroe," and then to his deputy headed for the door, "Let's get this show on the road."

Closing the door behind him, Sheriff Thompson stepped to the edge of the porch. Scanning the sea of familiar faces he began, "Okay people listen up, as you have all been informed, the two little Monroe girls, Jenna and Laci, are missing. We only have a few hours of daylight left. Each team leader has been given a radio and an area to be searched. If you find anything out of the ordinary, let your leader know, so they can radio it back to us here at base. We need to find them before dark or there will be two very cold, very hungry and very scared little girls out there. Okay, let's get going."

Popping a cigarette between his lips and striking a match, Dan leaned against the railing and tossed away the match. Drawing in deeply, he watched Laurel through the window as she was being interviewed by a detective.

He hated cases like this, ones involving kids. What was he dealing with? Two little girls who lost their way or......something else? Shaking the uneasy thought from his mind, Dan flicked his cigarette and headed down the steps crossing the yard to the trailer.

CHAPTER SEVEN

Lily Fernstat flipped the switch brightening the shadow-filled dining room as Detective Ted Brown and Laurel took a seat at the table. The cheery lemon yellow walls were embellished with an apple wallpaper border near the ceiling.

A large buffet with a silver tea service upon it was nestled along one wall and a china hutch holding all of Lily's best china was on the other. A long dining table with eight chairs centered the room with a frilly white lace table runner and two silver candlesticks adorning the top. The crystal chandelier hovering above the center of the room gave the essence of a Sunday meal about to be consumed rather than an interview to pinpoint the whereabouts of the two missing children.

"When was the last time you saw the girls, Mrs. Monroe?" Detective Brown asked Laurel.

"Last night, when I tucked them into bed."

"What time was that?"

"Ummm, 9:30 or so."

"It wasn't out of the ordinary for them not to be in bed when you woke up?"

"No, there are a lot of mornings, Jenna wakes up early and gets her sister up, they eat cereal and usually watch cartoons. I haven't been sleeping well lately and it's nice when she does that so I can sleep in." Lily sitting next to her, patted Laurel on the hand.

"So, you didn't find it unusual when the girls weren't watching television?" Detective Brown questioned.

"No, I didn't, they're very active little girls, detective, who love to play outside. They're very curious and love to explore. They love helping my brother with chores and when they weren't in the living room, I assumed they were outside,"

"Mrs. Monroe, you said you've been having trouble sleeping lately, is there a reason why?"

Seeing her daughter in desperate need of a break. "Would you like some coffee, detective?"

Laying his pencil aside. "Yes, thank you."

"Listen, Detective Brown, my ex-husband's a crazy bastard and intent on making my life a living hell. Instead of wasting your time questioning me, maybe you should be focusing your efforts on him!"

"LAUREL!" Lily hated the use of foul language in her house.

"I'm sorry mom, but you know as well as I do who's behind this whole thing," Laurel spit back.

Taking note of the venom in her voice, "Your ex-husband—Matthew Monroe?" the detective asked, studying Laurel's face.

"Yes! That's exactly who I'm talking about."

Glancing first at her mother, Detective Brown returned his gaze to Laurel. "I think we need to take a breather for a few minutes, why don't you get some fresh air, Mrs. Monroe."

As Dan stepped inside the trailer door, his eyes surveyed the room. There was by far nothing elaborate about the interior, but it was clean, well kept and a suitable place for a struggling single mother raising two small children. The kitchen and living room were separated by only the distinguishing line drawn on the floor where the carpeting of the living room met the linoleum of the kitchen.

The small open kitchen was to the right of the door and was furnished with only a Formica table and four chairs that had seen better days. The walls were covered with the dark wood paneling customary for older mobile homes such as this. The entire twelve foot width of the front kitchen was equipped with a countertop holding a coffee maker and toaster, cupboards, and a lone window overlooking the driveway and Lily Fernstat's house. The avocado stove and refrigerator which also were age appropriate lined the wall to the immediate right of the front counter. Although the kitchen was somewhat outdated, Dan noticed Laurel Monroe's attempt at making it homier, with cheery yellow curtains on the window and several needlepoint pictures depicting "Bless this Kitchen," adorning the walls.

Shaking his head, Dan turned and moved toward the door in search of a deputy. He wanted photographs of the inside before anything was disturbed.

Grateful for the break, Laurel rose from the table and made her way onto the front porch with Lily close on her heals. "Laurel, they're only doing their job."

"I know, mom, I am just worried sick about the girls, it's almost dark and you know how frightened they're going to be," she said, her eyes spotted the detective crossing the yard to the sheriff just coming out of her trailer.

"What did you get, Ted?"

"Dan, maybe we should bring Matthew Monroe in for questioning. I'm not finished interviewing her yet, but she mentioned him with more than a little animosity in her voice. I thought you might also want to be there for the rest of the interview."

"Let me get one of my deputies to pay Mr. Monroe a visit and I'll join you in the house." With that, Dan headed for a deputy standing nearby.

Sheriff Thompson removed his hat as he entered the house, noticing the worn out Laurel Monroe cradling her head in her hands. Moving across the room, he took a seat at the table.

"Mrs. Monroe, I know you're tired, but this is important in our finding Jenna and Laci. I've asked Sheriff Thompson to join us. Now, can you tell us about your ex-husband."

With a sigh, Laurel related to them all the sleepless nights and Matthews late night visits. The last visit he had and Jenna running out. Once she began, everything came spilling out.

"Why didn't you report any of this to the police?"

"You don't understand. MATTHEW IS CRAZY! He would've killed me if I had done that. I had to protect Jenna and Laci and I can't do that if I'm dead."

"Alright Mrs. Monroe, I want you to come with me over to your trailer. I want you to see if you can tell if anything is missing or if there is anything out of the ordinary. Walk me through what you did this morning so I can get an idea of what we are dealing with." Laurel nodded and allowed her mother to help her up.

Wrapping her arms around herself to ward off the chill creeping up her spine, Laurel followed the two men into the trailer. The emptiness of the place made her shiver. Lily gave her arm a reassuring squeeze.

Lily crossed the living room and turned on the one and only lamp, a floor lamp next to the couch. The sparsely furnished room was neat as a pin, showing no evidence of the two small children who lived there.

A lone tear slid down Laurel's cheek and she smiled sadly as the memory of her stubbing her toe that morning a few days before flooded her mind. She scanned the gold sculptured shag carpeting covering the floor which didn't so much as have a cookie crumb on it.

The patchwork quilt hiding the wear and tear of the old wood armed couch was neatly tucked in and the throw pillows were seemingly strategically placed in the corners. Besides the couch, the only remaining pieces of furniture were an older model television set, a glass-topped coffee table, and a small bookcase with doors hiding its contents.

Photographs of the girls in the various stages of their young lives were neatly hanging from the otherwise bare walls. White curtains trimmed with brown ruffles hung from the two windows of the room.

"Let's start in the bedroom, shall we?" The detective gestured for her to lead the way as he removed his notebook and pen from his pocket.

Lily lovingly nudged her daughter toward the hallway on the left side of the living room. A lump was beginning to form in the back of Laurel's throat as she led the others down the hall past the empty spare bedroom and bathroom on the right to her bedroom at the end.

The bedroom was not large by any stretch of the imagination. The full-sized bed was pushed against the far wall, with just enough space to open the door and a white crib was parallel to it, but at the opposite end and against the same wall as the door. At the end of the bed was just enough space to get to the built-in chest of drawers and closet. A white wicker hamper sat on the floor against the end of the crib, which with all of its pink and white frills was quite evident normally held a sleepy little girl .

Two windows provided light in the room, one of which was above the head of the bed and the other on the side of it. Bright blue and white checkered curtains hung from the windows, while the floor was covered with the gold carpet reminiscent of the living room.

Laurel began, "I was tired this morning, but the sun was in my eyes, so I got up. I told the girls I was taking a shower," as she spoke she moved from room to room reliving the events of that morning.

"Did they answer you?"

Thinking. "Ummm, I don't think so, I don't remember them answering, I just thought they were absorbed in cartoons. After showering, I headed into the living room. I noticed the television wasn't on and assumed they were outside. So, I went to the kitchen to start a pot of coffee and then made beds and picked up the bedroom." She stopped.

"Is something wrong?"

"There seems to be something, I just can't grasp it."

"Go on, maybe it will come to you."

Shaking herself, she went on, "I went back to the kitchen, poured myself some coffee and sat down. When I finished, I put the cup in the sink and became upset when I didn't see any cereal bowls in the sink. I thought Jenna had forgotten to feed Laci and that's when I went outside to bring them back in."

Standing in silence as Detective Brown finished taking notes, Laurel looked around the kitchen.

"Can you tell if anything is missing?"

Laurel shook her head as she wandered back down the hallway to the bedroom, closely followed by her mother and the two officers. She glanced around the room, letting her eyes rest on the crib. Crossing to the crib she rested her hands on the railing as she stared at the empty bed. Empty!

Snapping her head up. "Laci's meemee, Laci's meemee is gone."

"Her meemee?"

"Yes, yes, it's her favorite blanket. She can't sleep without it."

A puzzled frown shadowed the sheriff's face as he made a mental note of the discovery.

CHAPTER EIGHT

It was well past dark when the search was called off and the teams started arriving back at base. Sheriff Thompson thanked the volunteers, before sending them home to get some much needed sleep while the team leaders and deputies were sticking around to update him.

Gathering around the table, they highlighted areas on the map that had been searched. Nothing out of the ordinary was found. Chase sat at the table emotionally exhausted as he listened to the plans of tomorrows search, perking up as he heard mention of searching the nearby creek and orchard.

Folding the map. "Okay boys get some sleep and be back here at dawn."

Chairs scraped as everyone stood and headed for the door. Noticing Chase still seated at the table. "You better get some sleep too son," Gathering his papers and his hat, he patted Chase on the shoulder. Nodding, Chase got up and walked the sheriff to the door.

"We'll be back bright and early. Well, good night then."

"Good night and sheriff…Thanks."

"Don't be sayin thanks yet, we still have two little girls to find." With that he headed down the steps to his car, he had a long night ahead of him.

Back at the station, Dan removed his hat and hung it on the coat rack inside his office. Shuffling through the messages on his desk and not seeing anything pressing, he walked to the coffee pot.

Wiping a hand down his tired face, he poured himself a cup. Carefully sipping, good and strong, perfect.

A deputy popping his head in the door. "Boy, you look like crap."

"Thanks, I love you too."

"Sorry sir, uhh Matthew Monroe's in a room down the hall." Hearing this bit of information, Dan took another sip and headed for the door.

Matthew Monroe was six feet two inches of rugged, good-looking maleness. His square jaw, dimpled cheeks, and amethyst colored eyes, along with his thick, curly, black hair bestowed on him the ability to have any woman he wanted. The trouble was there was only one he did want and the bitch screwed things up. Sooner or later, though, she'd realize the error of her ways and of this he was certain. Yep, sooner or later!

Dan snarled upon entering the room at Monroe's smugness. Dan, himself, had never been handsome in the male model sense, but he'd never sent women scrambling to get away either. On the other hand, the lone man sitting at the table with his sparkling white teeth and bad boy charm made things hard for men like Dan. "Cocky son-of-a-bitch," he muttered as he walked over and rested his hip on the edge of the table.

"Matthew Monroe?"

"Yeah," Matthew nodded.

"What do you know about your daughters disappearance?"

"I have no idea what you're talkin about, Sheriff." Leaning back in his chair and locking his hands behind his head, Matthew drawled smugly.

Pounding his fist on the table. "Come on Monroe, your daughters, Jenna and Laci. When was the last time you saw them?"

Snapping upright. "Umm, uh, the other day I stopped by, I saw Jenna, but the little one was sleepin'."

"The little one? You don't know your daughters name, Monroe?"

"Shit, sheriff, I don't even know if that kid's mine. Besides, I don't see em very often."

"Yeah you sure are in the running for father-of-the-year. We're gonna be here all night, Monroe, unless you tell me where those girls are?"

"I DON'T KNOW. Why would you think I have anything to do with it?"

Pausing. "Your ex-wife says the last time you were there you had an incident involving Jenna. And then there's your late night visits."

Running his fingers through his hair. "Look the kid was playin' with a knife, of course, I'm gonna punish her. Every time I go over there the kid is in my face, she needed to learn respect. As for the late night visits, I'm remarried and I'm not out runnin' around at night."

Getting up, Dan walked around the table. "Laurel says you've been raising a ruckus outside at night and trying to break in." Sitting back in his chair, Matthew started laughing.

"You finding something funny?" Dan spit, disgusted with Matthew Monroe's outburst.

Still chuckling, Matthew straightened up. "I'm sorry, sheriff, but we're talkin' about the Queen of Paranoia here. My ex-wife always has and always will think there's someone out to get her. When we was married, she drove me nuts, she couldn't pass a window without spotting someone on the street, and she just "knew" they were up to no good. She hid behind curtains watchin' until they left. You'd think that woulda been the end of it, but no sir, not Laurel, once they left, she was afraid they were gonna "sneak up on her" by comin from a different direction." Pausing for a moment, Matthew asked for a cigarette.

Lighting it he went on, "If the key slid in the lock of the door "too easy", she "knew" someone was inside. When we were first separated, I tried to get her back and I did pay her late night visits, but that's a long time ago," smiling he said, "and believe me, Sheriff Thompson, she sure wasn't complainin'. No siree, she was enjoyin' it as much as I was." Matthew Monroe gestured with his eyebrows to drive his point home.

The deputy poked his head in the room motioning to speak with Dan. He re-entered the room with a perplexed look and said, "Okay,

Romeo, you're free to go, for now, but don't be goin' to far I may have more questions for you, soon." Matthew snubbed out his cigarette and left.

Scratching the back of his head as he left the room, Dan caught up with the deputy. "What the hell do you mean, Laurel Monroe called? What exactly did she say?"

"She said 'he's back', her ex-husband was outside trying to get in. She sounded terrified, sheriff, so I dispatched a car to drive over there and check it out. I just got a radio back from him, he said he didn't see anything or anyone around."

What the hell was going on here? Dan had the feeling he was being played, but the question was—By who?

CHAPTER NINE

Unable to rid his mind of the previous days events, Dan Thompson spent what was left of his night tossing and turning. Finally giving up, he tossed the covers aside, got out of bed, and shuffled his way to the kitchen to brew a pot of coffee. After showering and dressing, he filled his thermos and made his way back to the Fernstat farm.

Dan had been going over details and was walking the area around the trailer looking for evidence of last nights visitor when Detective Brown arrived.

"You're here early." Noticing the troubled look on the sheriff's face. "What's wrong?"

"I don't know, something just ain't right, Ted. We got a call late last night from Laurel Monroe about her ex-husband outside trying to get in."

"Matthew Monroe was here?" Ted Brown couldn't believe his ears.

"That's just it, Ted, when she called, Matthew Monroe was down at the station being interviewed by Yours Truly. I don't know what the hell is goin' on."

"WHAT?" Detective Brown exclaimed in stunned disbelief.

"Yeah, that's what I've been askin' myself all night long."

Dan left it at that as he looked to the sky and realized dawn was fast approaching. Turning at the sound of crunching gravel, he left

Ted with his thoughts as he went to greet the first of the arriving search teams.

Word had spread of the missing Monroe girls and more and more people came to help. Friends, neighbors, and complete strangers poured into the yard to assist in any way possible.

Standing on the porch, Lily's hand went to her throat, overwhelmed by the sight unfolding before her, the cars lining the road reached as far as her eyes could see.

Letting the door fall shut behind him, Chase, mouth gaping, walked up and put a hand on her shoulder. "People really do care about them, don't they?"

Lily sniffled, wiping a tear from the corner of her eye with her apron. "They sure do, Chase, they sure do."

The yard was filled to overflowing with women busy setting up tables to serve food to the teams throughout the day; children, no matter how big or small, passed out drinks, continuously restocking the ice-filled tubs for later.

Giving her son a tear filled smile, she flitted down the steps and across the yard to offer her heartfelt appreciation and her assistance. Grateful for the opportunity to do something other than sit and wait as others searched for her granddaughters.

Chase followed her down the steps, but headed for the sheriff and the large group of men preparing to head out.

"I want to thank everyone for their support in our search for Jenna and Laci. Because of the vast response, we'll now be able to cover more territory and work in shifts." Dan paused as his gaze fell on a mysterious woman standing to the back of the crowd and desperately trying to blend in. Fully aware of the sheriffs eyes on her she quickly pulled the collar of her tan jacket closer around her neck and made sure her dark glasses were covering her eyes before slipping quietly away as the sheriff once again turned his attention back to the task at hand. "After four hours, one team will return to eat and drink and the next crew will head out in their place. The first shift teams can go. Second shift teams, please come closer and I'll get you set up with instructions on what I need from you." Half of the men grabbed bottles of water and headed out in teams, Chase among them.

The rest gathered around Dan as he gave search instructions of buildings and roadside ditches, instructing them to be back in two hours for a bite to eat before their shift began.

Watching the second shift team spread out, Dan forgot about the odd woman when he caught sight of Lily Fernstat as she busied herself setting plates and silverware on one of the many tables.

Seeing him approach she asked, "Can I get you something, Sheriff Thompson? Some food maybe?

"Maybe a cup of that coffee there.... and a minute of your time." Lily poured a cup and handed it to him. Turning to let one of the ladies know she would be right back, she joined Dan on the other side of the table.

As they strolled the grounds she was humbled by the flurry of activity going on around them. "It's so heart warming to know you've so many people to call friend when the chips are down."

"Yes it is, there are a lot of people here determined to find those two little girls." Strolling a bit farther he broached the subject, "Mrs. Fernstat can you tell me about Laurel and Matthew's relationship?

"Their relationship? Matthew's a very possessive man, sheriff. When Laurel first found out she was pregnant, oh my, he just went ballistic." Playing with the pendant of her necklace she went on with tears in her eyes as she filled the sheriff in on the details of Laurel and Matthew's marriage. Dan stopped her after she spoke of Matthew's becoming a patient in a mental hospital.

"She had him committed?" Dan didn't realize things between the Monroes were so bad.

Lily nodded and went on, "Then after they were divorced Laurel was awarded full custody of Jenna, which came as no surprise to us. Laurel and the baby moved into the trailer here on the farm. Things got better with Matthew for awhile and I think Laurel became smitten with him again. I know she doesn't think I know, but I do. I'd see Matthew arrive late at night and leave before anyone was up and Laurel started smiling again, but she never mentioned

Matthew's nightly visits. That was until she found out she was going to have Laci."

"What happened then? You also mentioned his family harassing Laurel, were you talking his parents?" Dan urged hanging on every word out of Lily's mouth.

"They were part of it, but most of the harassment came from Matthew's twin brother, Michael."

"Twin brother? Matthew Monroe has a twin brother?" Dan didn't like the sound of this.

Lily nodded before continuing, "Then one day she came to me and told me that Matthew broke in and raped her. I really don't know what happened to be honest with you, but after she found she was pregnant they had their final falling out. Matthew remarried a few months ago, but he's still very resentful of Jenna and takes his anger out on her so bad it breaks my heart. Well, Sheriff Thompson I guess that's about it."

"Mrs. Fernstat, I wanna again assure you we are gonna find them, but I also wanna thank you for sharing' this with me. The more insight I have into the past, the better chance I have of finding Jenna and Laci, and whoever's responsible." Dan felt bad for Lily, he could tell how much she loved her granddaughters.

"Thank you, Sheriff Thompson." Lily rose and started back to the tables as she caught sight of the first of the search teams returning.

This thing just keeps getting deeper he thought as he blew out a deep breath and found his way to the returning group.

The exhaustion was apparent on Chase's face as Dan stood watching him unsaddle his horse. "How'd things go out there this morning?"

Chase shook his head in defeat as he led his horse to the water trough. "There's just no sign of them anywhere.... it's as if they don't even exist. We didn't even find as much as a foot print down by the creek, I know that's a good thing, but if we could just find something to tell us what direction to look at least then we'd feel as if we're accomplishing something." Exasperated he headed for the tables to get some food.

Forcing down his own frustration, Dan returned his thoughts to Laurel. He hadn't seen her yet today and needed to speak with her. Seeing the detective sipping a cup of coffee and speaking with one of the volunteers he decided now was as good a time as any.

Patting the volunteer on the back and thanking him for his help, Dan asked, "You got a minute, Ted?"

"Sure what's up?" Ted replied as he excused himself.

"Have you seen Laurel Monroe today?"

"No, I've been told she's resting, why you ready to talk to her?"

"Yeah, but first I wanna fill you in on the conversation I had with her mother and then we can both talk to her."

Gesturing for Ted to have a seat, Dan filled him in about the Monroe's relationship and his interview with Matthew. Ted's cell phone started ringing as soon as Dan finished relating the story, holding up a hand for him to hold on, he took the call.

Closing his phone, he turned to Dan. "I'm afraid I've been called away on another case, Dan. I'm sorry to leave you with such a mess."

"It's okay Ted, I've got it from here."

"Well at least let me go with you to talk to Mrs. Monroe first." Dan nodded and stood as they made their way to the trailer to speak with Laurel.

CHAPTER TEN

Laurel raised her chin and let the water pelt her in the face; the hot shower felt wonderful and allowed her to be alone with her thoughts. Her mind went to Matthew's visit last night—God, the man has balls the size of Texas. She figured of all nights, last night would be the one night he would leave her alone, but not Matthew. No, he was determined not only to take Jenna and Laci from her, but to flaunt it by continuing to torment her. If her call to the sheriff didn't prove he was crazy, she didn't know what would.

He was everywhere, she could smell him, she could sense him. She bent her head forward and allowed the water to run off the end of her nose in an attempt to wash him away.

Turning the faucet off, she toweled herself dry, and wrapped it around her as she stepped from the shower. Wiping the steam from the mirror, she stared at her reflection as she remembered her last meeting with Matthew..."You're mine, Laurel, you'll always be mine..."

Laurel jumped, catching her breath in her throat when she saw him approach her from behind in the mirror. Peering into her eyes, he smiled menacingly as he reached and unwrapped her towel, letting it fall to her feet. Eyes wide with fright, her heart pounded wildly as she watched him fondle and trace the knife blade around the nipple of her breast.

"Where are your precious little brats now, Laurel?" he whispered as he undid his zipper. Kissing the nape of her neck, he forced her eyes to watch him in the mirror, "Huh? I told you I would not share you with anyone, Laurel."

Gathering all the strength she could muster, she flew at him, screaming and fists flailing, "Noooooooooo."

Dan and Ted were just entering as the blood-curdling scream and the sound of breaking glass echoed through the trailer. Pulling his gun, Dan Thompson skillfully ran down the hallway with the detective on his heels.

Approaching the bathroom, Dan threw open the door with his gun at the ready. Stunned and mouth agape, he found Laurel Monroe lying on the floor wrapped only in a towel, blood seeping from the wounds on her hands.

Dropping to a knee next to her. "What happened, Mrs. Monroe? Are you okay? Turning to Ted. "Get some towels, she's bleeding pretty bad and get her mother in here."

Dan Thompson turned his attention back to Laurel. "Can you stand up, Laurel? We need to get you out of this pile of glass." Nodding she allowed him to grip her by the upper arms and lift her from the broken shards.

The detective with clean towels in his arms appeared at the door to the bathroom along with a shocked Lily Fernstat. "Laurel, my god, what happened to you?"

"Mrs. Fernstat, why don't you help her get dressed and meet us in the other room."

After helping Laurel dress, Lily led her to a chair in the kitchen and set out to find a first aid kit. Dan Thompson looked at Laurel's hollow expression with concern and glanced at Ted.

"What happened in there, Laurel?"

Slowly raising unsettlingly haunted eyes to him, she whispered loudly, "He was in there, he was in the bathroom." Lily came into the room and began cleaning the cuts on her daughters hands.

"Who was in the bathroom, Laurel? Matthew?"

Laurel's horrified eyes quickly filled with unshed tears as she nodded. "Yes, he was there when I stepped from the shower. He came up behind me when I was brushing my hair," sobbing she continued, "he took my towel off and I thought he was going to. ."

Dan raised a questioning eyebrow in Ted Brown's direction before turning to Laurel. "He took your towel off?"

"Yes and then he asked me where my girls are now?" Concerned, Lily stopped cleaning Laurel's wounds and looked at the sheriff.

"He WHAT?" Dan got up from his chair and returned to the bathroom to have another look around. Ted Brown scraped his chair against the floor of the kitchen and joined him.

"What do you think, Dan?"

"Hell, I don't know," Dan replied scratching the back of his head as he looked around, "There's no windows in here that he could have slipped out of." Gesturing toward the hall and bedroom, "and there is no way anyone could go out those windows, they crank open."

Squeezing his lip between his thumb and forefinger in thought, Dan spoke out loud, "I'm gonna get a couple of deputies in her to pull this place apart. If he's hiding in here, we'll find him."

Lily had finished bandaging Laurel's hands by the time the sheriff returned to the kitchen. She watched as the two deputies headed for the rear of the trailer in search of evidence of Matthew Monroe having been there.

By the time he returned to his seat at the table, Laurel Monroe had pulled herself together and the trance-like state all but disappeared from her eyes.

Lifting vengeful eyes to the sheriff. "Did you even attempt to arrest Matthew last night?" She went on before he could answer, "Obviously not or he wouldn't have been here this morning, would he?"

"Mrs. Monroe, Laurel, I couldn't arrest him last night." Dan said as he warily shifted his eyes to Ted.

Watching his eyes shift made Laurel nervous. "What do you mean? What's wrong?"

"Mrs. Monroe are you sure someone was at the door last night?"

Laurel looked from the sheriff to the detective and back again in disbelief. "What do you mean, Am I sure? Of course I'm sure and I'm also sure of who was at my door."

"Well, Mrs. Monroe, if there was someone there, it wasn't your ex-husband. He was at the station when your call came in, he was being questioned by me."

"Are you saying I'm lying, Sheriff Thompson?" Laurel was having a hard time keeping her cool.

"I'm not sayin' that at all, what I am sayin' is you've been under a lot of stress and pressure the last couple of…."

Laurel abruptly stood and stormed to the counter, taking a deep breath. "You think I'm imagining it, then. Well that's just great." With her wounded hands firmly planted on the counter and her back to them. "You know, I always knew he'd get himself out of this somehow, someway."

Turning around. "I don't know how, but I guarantee you Matthew Monroe had something to do with last night and he does have something to do with the girls' disappearance."

"Mrs. Monroe, Laurel, please calm down and have a seat."

"I don't want to have a seat, detective. I want you to believe me, I am NOT, I repeat NOT imagining this."

Dan sat silent pondering his next move. "There is something we can try, I hope we don't have to because I hope to find the girls before then."

Interested, Laurel sat back down and leaned forward as she intently listened to Sheriff Thompson formulate his plan.

CHAPTER ELEVEN

Emily Plackart smiled brightly as she handed a heaping plate of food to Chase. "How's that for a hungry man?.... .Hi Chase."

Chase's heart skipped a beat as his head snapped up at the sound of her voice. "Emily," Chase softly let her name roll from his lips, "when did you get back?"

He had never met anyone like Emily before, she was beautiful with her chocolate brown eyes and long flowing brown hair he dreamed of one day running his fingers through. Emily Plackart was not only the prettiest woman he had ever met, but also the most kind-hearted and so so so innocent. But that had ended as quickly as it began four years ago when she moved away.

"Two days ago, I couldn't stay away, I just love this place and....everything I've ever wanted is here...." she replied leaving the statement hanging heavily in the air.

Calming his wildly beating heart. "Well, umm, thanks for the food, Emily, and umm it's real nice having you back." Flashing her a dimpled grin, he turned and went in search of a place to sit, reminding himself there would be plenty of time to reconnect with Emily after this was all over.

Catching her own breath, Emily watched Chase take a seat next to his sister and the sheriff. She hadn't realized the depth of her feelings for Chase until seeing him again.

Dan nodded to him as Chase took a seat next to Laurel. "We still have several hours of daylight yet, Mrs. Monroe. Is there any place out of the ordinary you can think of that maybe we haven't checked? Any little hidin' places the girls like, maybe?"

Laurel sat staring in the direction of the pasture. "No, I've been racking my brain for such things, but there are none that I can think of."

Cautiously watching her hypnotic state, Chase followed her eyes to the pasture lying just outside of the barn and then back to her. Pulling his eyes from Laurel's face, Chase looked at the sheriff, who also had a look of concern. "Umm, I can't think of any place either, we've checked every where around here."

Rising from his seat, Dan excused himself and headed toward the barn and pasture Laurel Monroe had been so mesmerized with.

"Laurel maybe you need to go lay down for awhile."

"No, I'm okay, I just wanna sit here for awhile yet." Never moving her eyes.

Finishing his food, Chase took one last drink and got up, "Well, I'm going to head back out. You really should think about getting some rest, sis." Tossing his plate in the trash, Chase headed for the barn and his horse, worrying about the toll this was taking on her.

Watching Chase head in the direction of the orchard, Dan rubbed his chin and turned his attention to the area around the barn and nearby pasture. What did Laurel Monroe find so interesting down here? Was she experiencing mothers intuition or was she just losing it?

CHAPTER TWELVE

Chase was frozen in his saddle hearing the shouts from two volunteers, "I think we've got something over here."

A short stocky deputy radioed back to base as he dismounted his horse, "Hey sheriff, I think we've found something," the unmistakable smell of decomp weighed heavily in the air as he added, "and by the smell of it, it ain't gonna be good."

"Keep Chase away until you've had a chance to check it out," Dan's voice squawked back.

Chase's eyes were glued to the thicket of underbrush, he and Jenna had visited earlier in the week. A grim expression settled on his face, his shoulders slumped, and a tear slid down his cheek as the sheriff's voice filled the air.

Coming to his senses, he dismounted and plowed his way through a group standing near the thicket. "Grab him," the stubby deputy yelled, "Chase, you can't go down there."

The dark menacing look in his eyes, caused the deputy to take a step back. "Deputy, if you know what's good for you, you'll kindly take your hands off of me." Without moving his eyes from the profusely sweating deputy, Chase jerked his arm free and headed for the brush.

"Are you sure you want to be here, Chase?" asked the volunteer who made the discovery as he sat squatting outside of the thicket.

Chase tore his eyes from his and focused on the mass of underbrush as a voice rented the air from inside, "False alarm, boys, it's just a coon carcass caught in a trap."

Laying his head back Chase allowed the warm afternoon sun beat against his face as he let out a pent up sigh of relief, silently thanking God.

Chase returned just as it was getting dark, he saw the last of the volunteers heading up the road. The sheriff was at the house drawing up plans for tomorrow before heading out. Dismounting, he led his horse into the barn and began removing the saddle.

Giving the horse water and hay, Chase set to brushing it. At the sound of light footsteps, he turned and suddenly found himself drowning in the chocolate pools of Emily Plackart's eyes.

"You look like someone who needs someone to talk to," she said peering deeply into his sapphire eyes, "or at least a shoulder to cry on."

Chase smiled sadly as Emily rested her palm on his cheek. "Do you want to talk about it?"

Nodding Chase took the blanket from her arms and spread it on the ground outside of the barn. Taking her hand he helped her to the blanket and took a seat next to her.

Emily studied his profile as he sat gazing at the stars Chase took a deep breath as he rested his arms on his bent knees. "It's such a big world out there and they're so small."

Emily brushed a lock of his sandy hair from his forehead. "I know."

Turning to look into her eyes. "Have you met someone?" he asked afraid of the answer.

Shaking her head, her eyes never left his. "No one has ever been able to measure up to you, Chase. You stole my heart four years ago and no matter how hard I've tried I've never gotten it back." She turned to look out over the pasture. "How about you, do you have someone else?"

Gripping her lightly under the chin he turned her face to him. "There's no one for me but you, Emily." Brushing a tear from her eye with his thumb. "It broke my heart to watch you walk out of my life back then and I told myself I'd never do it again."

Whispering, "I'm so sorry, Chase, I never intended to hurt you, but I had to take care of my mother, please don't be angry with me."

"I could never be angry with you, Emily." His lips found hers in a kiss so tender it took both of their breaths away. Leaving her lips, Chase left a trail of kisses down the side of her neck as he ran his fingers through her beautiful hair, whispering huskily against her ear, "God I've missed you, but I'm very close to losing control right now, so I better walk you to your car before things get out of hand."

Confused and hurt Emily searched his eyes as he planted a kiss on the end of her nose and smiled sheepishly. "I'm not a young boy anymore and I just don't want to rush things," he explained.

Nodding she understood, she took the hand he offered her. Chase helped her to her feet before pulling her into his arms. "Welcome home, Emily," he whispered against her hair.

Closing her eyes against his shoulder she felt a stirring deep within her as she said, "It's good to be home, Chase."

He kissed her on the top of her head before turning them toward the car. Chase kept an arm around her shoulder as they leisurely made their way up the hill.

Putting her arm behind him she gave him a reassuring squeeze. "Let's hope tomorrow brings better luck finding the girls." Reaching her car, Chase held the door as she got behind the wheel. Squatting outside the drivers window, "I'm really glad we had a chance to talk." Leaning through the car window, he kissed her goodnight.

Smiling as she headed down the drive, yes, she was definitely glad they did, too. Looking in her rearview mirror she saw Chase give her one last wave before heading for the house.

Sticking to the shadows, the dark figure crossed the yard, as he had so many nights before, quietly working his way to the trailer. Pausing as he reached the front, he scanned the trees and peeked around the corner. Seeing nothing, he inched his way around it and as quietly as possible moved up the steps. Hesitantly, putting his hand around the doorknob.

Suddenly finding himself flooded in bright light he slowly turned and threw an arm up to shield his eyes from the brightness. Laurel, standing next to the sheriff's car, dropped her arms to her sides in stunned disbelief and gasped, "Chase?"

CHAPTER THIRTEEN

All eyes were on Chase as he sat slump shouldered hanging his head at the table. "You've got some explaining to do, son." Sheriff Thompson was first to speak as Lily Fernstat poured coffee and took a seat between her son and daughter.

Laurel became hysterical, feeling violated, "How could you do something like this to me, Chase? It's been you all along, hasn't it? HASN'T IT?" Giving her brother a shove on the shoulder. "How could you, dammit? How could you torment and scare me like that night after night?"

"Woe, woe, calm down, Mrs. Monroe, calm down." Dan shot out of his chair to pull the ranting Laurel from her brother, "Now, sit down."

Turning his attention to Chase as he spoke, "It's not what you think, for god's sake Laurel I'd never do anything to intentionally hurt you. I'm sorry I scared you, hell, I didn't even know you were aware I was out there."

"Then exactly what were you doing out there?" Dan was determined to get to the bottom of this.

Sighing, Chase blew out a breath and closed his eyes for a second as the burden settled on his shoulders. "I know how frightened of Matthew you are Laurel. I hate seeing that fear on your face, so just to satisfy myself that you're okay, I check to make sure you lock the door every night. I also walk around to make sure the bastard isn't hiding anywhere." Chase tried to take his sister's hand, Laurel pulled back.

"After your divorce, I found Matthew coming down from the porch late one night. He became flustered when he saw me and I figured he was up to no good. Once he left I checked your door and have every night since. I have never told you of the incident because I didn't want to scare you anymore than you already were. I guess I was wrong to not tell you, I'm sorry.

"I don't understand how you couldn't have known how frightened I have been during the night. It's not like it has been a secret." She shrugged, "I have talked to mom about it many times and the sheriff just a couple of days ago," Laurel spoke in a low unsettling tone that worried Lily along with the hollow look in her daughter's eyes.

"I don't know either, I must never have been around at the times you discussed it. I surely would have come clean and…"

"It doesn't matter, Matthew still has something to do with all of this. All I wanted to do was protect my girls. I'd do anything I could to keep them safe…"

Her last statement sent chills down Sheriff Dan Thompson's spine, and he had the feeling there was more meaning behind her words than the obvious.

No longer able to sit and watch her daughter have a meltdown, Lily brought an end to the conversation. "I think that's more than enough for tonight," helping Laurel to her feet, "come on dear, let's get you into bed, you'll feel better after you've had some sleep."

Watching Lily help her daughter down the hallway, Dan heard, "I only want to protect them. I only want to keep them safe." He knew he was witnessing the mental breakdown of Laurel Monroe.

Motioning for Chase to follow, Dan picked up his hat and headed for the front porch. Taking a seat on the top step, he removed a cigarette and struck a match. Chase taking a seat next to him declined the sheriff's offer to join him in a smoke.

Taking the time to thoroughly enjoy his smoke, Dan considered the best way to approach Chase with his concerns. Flicking his cigarette, he continued to watch the red glow until it was no longer visible.

"Chase," he began, "I don't think I have to tell you what a fragile state your sister is in right now."

"No you don't, I can see she's on the verge of cracking." Leaning back on his elbows, Chase looked at the stars.

Dan took a deep breath before proceeding. "Look, I've got some thoughts I wanna share with you, but I need you to hear me out and try to listen objectively. Okay?"

Sparking his interest, Chase dropped his gaze to the sheriff's face and sat up resting his arms on his knees. "I'm all ears, Dan, what are ya thinking?"

"Chase, this is going to sound way out there, but....do you think Laurel could've had anything to do with the girls disappearance," there he said it.

Speechless, Chase stared at Dan in stunned disbelief. "Laurel? Are you crazy, Dan? Those girls are her entire life, what on earth would lead you to believe she could possibly hurt them?"

"I know, I know, it sounds ridiculous, but let's look at what we know and look at it with an open mind. Please, okay?"

Reluctantly, Chase nodded. "Okay, then, I interviewed Matthew Monroe last night, he says after the divorce he did pay your sister visits at night. But not in an attempt to hurt her. According to him he was still very much in love with her and they were having secret rendezvous' trying to reconcile."

"But Laurel said he raped her, I for one believe her, and you..."

"You agreed to keep an open mind." Pausing to make sure Chase had himself under control, he continued, "just think back to the night you caught him leaving the porch. Are you sure he was trying to get in and failed? Or could he have been inside with Laurel and was leaving so as not to cause her any grief?" Dan questioned.

"Then there's Laci's blanket."

"Laci's blanket? What does that have to do with anything?"

"Laurel discovered Laci's favorite blanket missing from her crib. She called it...I don't know...her meemee or...Something like that."

Searching Dan's face for an answer. "I still don't understand why that makes you think it's Laurel."

"Don't you see? If Matthew Monroe was the one who took the girls, he isn't the type to worry about the little girls comfort. He says he doesn't even know if she's his and with his resentment for Jenna, he doesn't strike me as a man who likes kids. Why would a man who doesn't like kids think to grab the child's favorite blanket? That sounds more like something only a mother would think of."

As things started to take hold in Chase's mind, he rubbed his hands down his face, "But why would Laurel do that?"

Lighting another smoke, Dan said, "I think she gave us the answer inside just a little while ago."

Replaying the scene from inside just moments before, Chase asked, "What do you mean?"

"She said she wanted to protect them and keep them safe. She has herself believing Matthew was the one trying to break in. She may have also convinced herself he wanted to take them away from her. The only way she could protect them was to hide them."

"But if that is the case, why would she let it go this far?" Chase pointed out.

"Hell, I don't know, maybe with all of the stress she's under and the lack of sleep, she doesn't remember doing it. Or.....maybe she is trying to make us all believe it was Matthew, so he would once and for all be out of her life." Dan hoped it was the former, because he hated to think Laurel Monroe could be as vindictive as the latter suggested.

Things were finally falling into place. "God, I feel so damn bad for putting her through this. But, geez, I was only trying to watch out for her...If what you say is true, how are we going to find them?"

"I don't know, but I also can't shake the feeling they are right under our noses."

"Yeah, I feel the same way, as if I should know where, but can't put my finger on it," Chase added.

"Well, I guess we'll figure that out tomorrow, I'm gonna go home and try to get some sleep. I suggest you do the same. See ya in the morning." With that Dan headed for his car and his much needed bed.

Chase's thoughts were far from sleep, Could it be Laurel? He needed to see Emily, he needed her to comfort him and tell him everything was going to work out. Convincing himself that was all he had on his mind, he got into his truck and headed for Emily's.

CHAPTER FOURTEEN

The sight of her standing inside the door took his breath away. Opening the screen she said, "Chase? What is it? What's wrong?"

"I...I...I don't know, I just had to see you. Some things happened tonight and I don't know, I just needed to hold you," he stammered.

Slipping easily into his arms. "Things? What things?"

"We can talk about it later. Right now I just want to hold you." He could already feel his loins stirring to life as he bent his head and found her lips.

Coming to his senses, Chase removed her arms from around his neck. "You need to watch yourself, Emily, I told you earlier, you're not dealing with a young boy anymore and if you keep this up I can't guarantee you won't end up with more than what you bargained for. You have no idea what you are doing to me right now." Chase closed his eyes and took a deep breath bringing his emotions in check.

Emily left his arms and walked to the door, closed and locked it before turning to Chase. "I know you are not a boy anymore, just as I am no longer a school girl, Chase."

The fire burning in her eyes matched the one in his groin spark for tantalizing spark as he closed the distance between them. Chase swept her off her feet and headed down the hall following Emily's directions to the bedroom as she sprayed his cheek and neck with feather-light kisses.

"Geez, woman, stop that or I'm not even gonna make it to the bedroom," he grunted huskily.

Inside the room, he laid her gently on the bed before removing his boots and joining her. He sent a bolt of lightning shooting through her as he untied her robe and found her breast. Pulling his lips from hers, Chase got up from the bed to remove his own clothing.

Her robe discarded, Emily kneeled on the edge of the bed in her beautiful nakedness to help him. Emily could see in his eyes he needed her to comfort him, she did just that. Showering his chest with cotton soft kisses, she worked at his belt. Freeing it, she continued her way to the buttons on his shirt, following her fingers with the soft tickle of her tongue.

Emily let her gaze capture his as she slid his shirt off his shoulders letting it fall to the floor. Tearing her eyes from his, she tantalizingly unzipped his jeans, freeing his manhood for her to fully explore. Chase stepped out of the pants at his ankles as Emily stepped from the bed and dropped to her knees.

Throwing his head back, he gripped hers in his hands as her tongue played magic on his senses. "Oh god, Emily, oh my god."

Pulling her up to stand in front of him. "You have to stop, you don't know what you are doing, I can't hold back much longer with you doing that," Chase slowly and deliberately caressed every inch of her as he once again laid her gently on the bed. Parting her legs, he rose above her gazing deeply into her eyes as he entered her in one swift movement.

Emily screeched and Chase stopped, searching her eyes. "I'm sorry, Emily, I thought you…I mean I didn't know you never…"

Kissing his chin and smiling. "I told you no one measured up to you, and I meant it."

Heart warming to her words, he slowly moved himself in and out as he kissed every inch of her face. Pulling himself out, he kissed and fondled her breasts, teasing her nipple with his tongue and slowly began his descent to her womanhood. Emily gasped as he tortured her with his gentle caressing hands.

With fire in his eyes he moved over her and plunged himself deep into her womanly sheath. Moving together in a fevered frenzy until they both free fell into oblivion.

Relaxed and totally satisfied, they laid together as she rested her head on his chest. Circling his nipple with her finger, Emily asked, "So, what happened tonight, Chase?"

Twirling a strand of her beautiful hair between his fingers, he related to her the events of the evening.

Raising her head to look into his eyes. "Oh my god. What do you think? Could it be?"

Chase sighed, "You know, I don't know what to think anymore. I never would've imagined Laurel doing it. And I didn't believe it when he first suggested it, but the more I've thought about her erratic behavior, the more I think he may be right."

Tears in her eyes. "I am so sorry, Chase. I wish there was something I could do to help you."

Chuckling and hugging her tightly. "You already have, sweetheart, you already have." Yawning and holding her close, Chase fell into a deep and restful sleep.

Waking well before dawn, Chase studied Emily's sweet face with long eyelashes brushing her cheek, wondering, What did I do to deserve you, Emily Plackart?

Remembering the joy and pleasure she brought to him last night, his hand massaged first her tummy and then lowered to the triangle of curls.

"Mmmm, you're up early." Stretching, she snuggled closer to his side.

"Hmm, hmm, it's hard to sleep laying so close to something so beautiful and so, so sexy. Besides I was hoping for a little treat before I leave." When he shined his dimples, Emily became putty in his hands.

Emily rose on one elbow, kissing his eyelids and lowering her hand to stroke the already bulging evidence of his love.

Grabbing her hand. "Uh uh, sweet thing." He gently rolled her to her back and showed her how much he loved her.

"You are insatiable," she teased playfully as she threw the covers aside and donned a robe.

"Yes, I am, when it comes to you," he said as he wiggled his eyebrows.

Throwing a pillow in his direction. "I'm going to start some coffee, the shower is in there if you want."

"Are you going to join me?" he hinted.

"You're terrible, Chase." Emily ruffled his hair as she re-entered the bedroom. "Besides, there will be plenty of time for us after we find the girls."

Snapping back to reality, he hopped out of bed and headed for the shower. "You're right, I need to get going."

Grabbing his arm as he passed. "I nothing. We need to get going."

His eyes warmed. "You want to go with me? You don't have…"

She interrupted, "I want to Chase, I want to be there for you." Hugging her, she slapped him on the behind. "Now, get in the shower or I'm leaving without you."

CHAPTER FIFTEEN

Laurel Monroe's mental state worsened, dark circles under her eyes became increasingly evident. She sat staring and rambling about keeping the girls safe. Lily was distraught with worry over Laurel's deteriorating condition.

"Mom, we need to call a doctor, she is having some kind of breakdown."

Covering her daughter's shoulders with a blanket, she rubbed her back. "I am going to make you some tea, dear."

Chase followed close on her heels as she headed for the kitchen. "Mom, we have to do this." Afraid to bring up their fears of her involvement, Chase paused. "Mom....we have to, Laurel may be the only one who knows where the girls are." Sucking his lungs full of air, he braced himself for his mothers reaction.

Whipping around to look into her sons face, Lily kept her voice to a loud whisper, "What are you talking about? Have you lost your mind, Chase?"

"Mom, mom, just listen." Grabbing her arm as she tried to walk away, Chase turned her around. "I will not listen to this, this is absurd." Pulling away, Lily busied herself making Laurel's tea.

"Mrs. Fernstat." Emily cautiously approached, gently cupping Lily's elbow. "Please, please just listen to Chase." leading Lily to a chair, Emily pulled one to sit close to her. "Mrs. Fernstat, if you don't want to listen for anyone else, please do it for Jenna and Laci."

Handing Lily a tissue to wipe away the lone tear slipping down her cheek. "Those two little girls are out there somewhere, alone.... And scared. Please, Mrs. Fernstat, for them?

The compassion in the beautiful young woman's eyes warmed Lily's heart, softly blowing her nose, she reluctantly nodded. "Okay," she whispered. Chase and the sheriff quickly took seats intent on getting their feelings across to Lily before she changed her mind.

"Mrs. Fernstat, Laurel may be losing her grip on reality." pausing Dan went on, "Remember the incident earlier in the bathroom?" Receiving a nod. "Laurel said Matthew removed her towel, but yet when we found her it was still wrapped around her and we found no evidence of him having been there."

Lily turned her attention to her son as he began to speak, "Mom, you know as well as I do that Matthew could care less about the girls. He's not going to want to bother with them."

"Chase, you don't know that for sure. What if he did just to get back at Laurel?"

"Mom, you are beginning to sound like Laurel, because don't you see, that's what she thinks too?" Chase looked to Emily and the sheriff for support.

Dan Thompson took the hint. "Mrs. Fernstat, we believe that may be what prompted her to do it. We think Laurel may have hidden the girls to protect them, and may not remember doing it."

Lily buried her face in her hands for a moment before she spoke, "I don't understand, why wouldn't she remember doing something like that with her children? She loves them more than anything in this world."

Having the same initial reaction, Chase explained, "She's been under so much stress, mom, with Matthew's infrequent visits, the girls being so active is a lot of work for her to handle alone, and...." Kicking himself for his role in the last part. "I sure didn't help matters by scaring her the way I did...,"

"Chase," Emily interjected, "you have to stop blaming yourself, you were protecting her, you had no idea."

"Emily's right, son, you had only the best intentions in mind." Dan could see how much Chase blamed himself for his sisters breakdown.

Lily hated to admit it, but she knew what they were saying made sense. "If this is the case, what do we do? How do we find the girls?"

Grateful for her cooperation, Dan let out a sigh. "First of all, we need to call a doctor, we don't want to do anything to make her condition worse. My guess would be, she'll be admitted to the hospital." Receiving a nod, Dan rose to make the call.

"Mom, we both know this is the right thing to do, not only for the girls sake, but Laurel's too."

Laying her hand on her sons cheek. "I know, Chase, I know, but it doesn't make it any easier, sweetheart." Rising from her seat, Lily went to see to her daughter.

Watching his mother leave the room, Emily rose to stand behind Chase, placing reassuring hands on his shoulders. "I know all of this must be really hard for her. I feel so helpless, I want to do something to help Laurel."

The spine chilling, blood curdling screams emanating from the living room brought Chase and Emily bolting from the other room. Chase caught sight of Dan Thompson's tall stature racing in the front door.

"What the hell…?"

Curled in a fetal position in the corner of the room was Laurel Monroe screaming, "Noooooooo, noooooooo." Her hollowed out eyes were spooked and empty.

Chase and the sheriff tried desperately to calm the demented screaming woman, but the effort was futile. She seemingly had taken on super human strength and every time they subdued her arms, her legs began kicking in a frenzy to free herself from unseen demons.

Emily took the distraught Lily into her arms to shield her from the horrifying display. Chase and Dan finally had her legs and arms under control as the paramedics came through the front door.

The sight of the two dark haired paramedics sent Laurel into another frenzied fit of violently kicking and screaming, "Noooooooooo, stay away from me. Do you hear me, staaaaayyyyy awwwaaaayyyy from meeee."

Gripping her arms more tightly to allow the paramedics to administer a sedative, Dan watched the tortured Laurel Monroe's chest heave in exhaustion. The two men helped get her body on the stretcher and strapped down as a precautionary measure.

Chase could hear the soft moaning sobs of his mother coming from behind. His eyes misted over as his shoulders sagged watching the empty shell that was once his sister taken out the front door to the waiting ambulance.

CHAPTER SIXTEEN

Standing on the front porch, Chase watched the ambulance pull away. His legs no longer able to support his weight, he took a seat on the steps. Resting his arms on his legs, he silently laced his fingers together. Sensing his need for reassurance, Emily quietly stepped behind him and gently massaged his shoulders

Breaking the silence as she continued kneading his shoulders. "Remember how the three of us played when we were little, the predicaments we got into?"

Remembering, he smiled and nodded solemnly. "Like the time before that old outhouse was torn down?"

Giggling. "Yes, exactly, I still can't believe your sister hid down inside there, yuck."

"You have to admit, in a game of hide and seek it was the best hiding spot there was." Chuckling at the memory and shaking his head. "I mean who would think to look down there?"

Emily was happy to take Chase's mind temporarily off of his sister's current state of mind. "Yeah, no kidding, what about the time that tornado was sighted near here, you remember that?" She asked patting him on the shoulder.

"Remember it? How could I forget it? I've never been more scared in my life, but not Laurel, remember? We were playing in the trailer…."

"Yeah and it was rocking so bad from the wind I thought it was going to tip over."

"Geez, it was, wasn't it, I thought it was going to blow away, but she tried convincing us if it did we would just pick it up and carry it back."

Laughing Emily recalled, "I was never so relieved as when your parents made us go down to the storm cellar. I was...."

Snapping his head. "What did you say?"

"I said I was relieved...Chase?"

"No, no, not that. The storm cellar...,my god, it hasn't been used in years."

"Chase, you don't think...."

"Well, we're gonna find out, c'mon." With legs instantly recovering Chase shot off the porch, running for the barn.

Dan, speaking with a volunteer, spotted Chase racing toward him. Grabbing his arm as he was about to pass. "What the hell's goin' on?"

Chase excitedly said, "Dan, I think I know where the girls are."

Searching Chase's face as if to see the answer written on it. "What? Where?"

"There's an old storm cellar, we haven't used for a long time,"

Prodding Chase to go on even though Dan knew the answer. "Where's it at?"

"Outside the barn in the pasture with the water trough." By this time Dan was running along side of him

"Why haven't we come across it? We've been over that ground I don't know how many times."

"The ground has pretty much become part of the door over the years and all that sticks up is a small loop. I don't know why I didn't remember it sooner, just the other day Jenna caught her toe on it and stumbled."

"Dan, we're gonna need flashlights."

Nodding, Dan took off to round up some men and get flashlights from the trunk of his car. Turning to Emily. "Sweetheart, go get mom and bring her down." hugging him, she turned to go. "And Emily…thank you." Smiling, she set off on her mission to retrieve Lily Fernstat.

CHAPTER SEVENTEEN

By the time Chase made his way to the barn and pasture, Dan Thompson had already gathered a group together. Dan motioned for Chase to join them and waited for him to approach.

"Okay, Chase, where do you want us?" Dan questioned looking for evidence of the loop Chase was talking about.

"It's over here," Chase said over his shoulder as he headed for the area next to the water trough. Emily and Lily were arriving just as Chase and the sheriff. Chase hugged and kissed Emily on the forehead as he squeezed his mother's arm. Releasing her, Chase bent to study the ground, Dan stooped next to him and searched for the loop.

Chase threw an arm in the air. "Sh, sh, did you hear that, Dan?"

He had also heard the muffled scream and frantically looked for the handle of the door. They knew they were close but something was drastically wrong. Chase moved the cement block he had watched Jenna drag to the water trough. There it was, so full of years of built up soil it no longer resembled a door. Chase pulled on the heavy door and laid it open.

The two men peered into the blackness. "Hand me a couple of those flashlights." Dan handed one of them to Chase.

"Jenna? Laci?" The only response was soft crying. "I'm going down."

Lily's heart was beating wildly. "Be careful, Chase."

Chase entered the hole and made his way down the steps, at the bottom he scanned the room with the light. He was not prepared for the sight the beam of his light caught.

Panicked. "Oh, god," He quickly closed the distance between them, going down on a knee he checked Laci for a pulse and getting a faint one. "Get an ambulance, get an ambulance," Chase screamed over his shoulder to Dan who was halfway down the steps.

When Dan yelled up to relay the frantic request, Lily Fernstat fell to her knees beside the hole and sobbed, "Chase, Chase, what is it?"

Chase looked into Jenna's tear-stained face. "Toad, are you okay, are you hurt?" He tried to force the panic from his voice and stay calm as he spoke to her as she sat cradling Laci's head in her lap. He didn't know the extent of his nieces injuries and didn't want to frighten Jenna, creating any sudden moves of the little ones neck.

Dan approached the scene as Chase was keeping Jenna calm; his stomach rolled when he saw the little ones face. Laci Monroe's forehead was deep purple and swollen so large it hung over her eyes giving her a monster like appearance.

Raising tear stained cheeks to her uncle, Jenna whispered, "I can't get her to wake up, Uncle Chase."

Rubbing a soothing hand down Jenna's mud streaked cheek. "What happened, kiddo?"

Her chest racking with sobs. "We were pushing as hard as we could, but the door wouldn't open. Then...then...Laci fell down the steps and...and...now I can't get her to wake up." Knowing Jenna was about to panic, he called for the sheriff.

"Dan." Realizing Chase had been calling his name, he dropped to the ground next to him.

Whispering to the sheriff, "We have to stabilize Laci's neck so we can get Jenna's legs out before she panics and jars it."

Nodding. "I'll hold her head still, you keep Jenna calm." Dan instructed Chase, knowing Jenna would remain calmer being handled by her uncle.

Chase moved closer to Jenna. "Toad, this is Sheriff Thompson,"

"Hi Jenna, it's nice to meet you, we've been looking for you, you are a very brave little girl." Looking at Chase, Dan nodded for him to continue.

"Okay, toad, Sheriff Thompson here is going to hold Laci's head. Okay? When he holds it, I want you to very carefully pull your legs out. Okay? Understand?"

Sobbing softly, Jenna nodded. Motioning to Dan he was ready, he returned his attention to Jenna. "Okay now remember, very slowly and very carefully."

Dan held Laci's swollen, lifeless head stable in his hands. Convinced that Dan had a good hold, Chase slid Jenna's legs free. Wrapping his arms around her, he buried his face in her hair as he stroked the back of her head and allowed his own tears to fall.

"You have no idea, little one, how scared we were." Sniffling and wiping his nose on his sleeve, he headed for the steps.

Above ground a couple of the men hollered, "People back up, give us some room, we've got one coming up." Reaching into the darkness, the two pulled Jenna to safety and the crowd erupted into cheers with the sight of the first lost child coming into view.

Lily's arms opened wide as Jenna was deposited gently onto her lap. Smothering the child's face with kisses, she hugged her tightly to her breast as people swarmed them ruffling Jenna's hair and patting each other on the back.

After handing Jenna up, Chase returned to Dan's side. "How bad is she?"

"I can't even begin to guess, but she looks bad. Get a blanket, we don't want her going into shock, Chase. Where the hell's that ambulance?"

Chase ran back to the steps. "Hey," he yelled, "We need some blankets down here."

The crowd above sobered quickly remembering there was yet another little girl to be rescued. Blankets retrieved from the barn were quickly passed through the crowd and down the opening to Chase's waiting hands.

A sharp beep, beep, beep announced the arrival of the ambulance; the sea of people parted to make room for the backing vehicle. Silence fell heavily as a backboard was lowered into the hole followed by the emergency personnel.

"Geez, what the hell happened?" exclaimed one of the paramedics as he knelt down beside her. The four of them effortlessly but carefully moved Laci's little body to the board. Starting an IV, one of the medical crew surveyed the injuries. "This is going to be tricky."

The other nodded in agreement. "We aren't going to be able to strap her head because of that injury." Discussing their options they settled on packing towels to either side of her head to stabilize it.

The crowd was completely hushed as Lily and Jenna were directed to wait in the ambulance. The emergence of the first paramedic out of the hole spurred several men forward to lend him a hand.

"I need some of you to help lift the board out of there. We want as little jarring as possible."

Everyone held their breath as the operation was conducted. Once above ground, the stretcher with Laci Monroe's battered little body was quickly and carefully loaded into the waiting ambulance along with her grandmother and sister.

Swallowing the lump, Chase cleared his throat as his gaze continued to follow the ambulance in route to the hospital.

Dan gripped his flashlight and lifted the beam to survey the underground room. Dark, dingy dirt walls and floor made him shudder to think of how frightened the two small girls must have been. The beam of light fell across a dirt encrusted pink blanket, "Her meemee," he whispered.

Moving the light across the floor it fell on several empty water bottles and crumpled snack wrappers. Shaking his head, he picked up the child's beloved blanket and headed for the steps as he muttered, "How could something like this happen?"

Spotting Dan emerge from the hole in the ground, Chase and Emily approached. Handing the blanket to Chase. "I found Laci's meemee."

Turning the filthy piece of cloth in his hands. "Dan, what's going to happen, now? Will Laurel be charged?"

"Right now Chase I can't say, it's very possible she will. Right now though you should concentrate on the girls. Go, go to the hospital, I'll finish things up around here."

Putting an arm around Emily, they started heading for his truck, pausing, Chase turned back, smiling. "Oh and sheriff.....thanks."

Remembering the first night of their search when he stopped Chase from saying those exact words, Dan shook his head and chuckled. "Don't mention it, now get out of here."

Dan Thompson's smile faltered as his gaze fell on the lone woman standing away from the crowd, watching the ambulance pull away. Studying her profile suspiciously, he couldn't help but notice the large dark glasses covering her eyes and cautiously made his way to her.

The unidentified woman in the dark glasses and tan jacket turned as the ambulance drove out of sight, coming face to chest with Dan. "Ma'am, is there something I can help you with?" asking as he gripped her arm.

The woman in tan quickly lowered her head as she sputtered. "Um, no, thanks anyway, though."

Holding her arm a bit tighter. "Maybe you need a ride and what kind of gentleman would I be not to offer a lady a ride." Dan was not about to let her slip away again without finding out how she was connected to this.

"Um, oh no, no sheriff I'm..."

"Oh, but I insist," Dan interrupted in a tone challenging her to stop him and she went with him without further resistance to his car.

At the station, Dan led her into a small room equipped with only a table and two chairs, then left to retrieve a female officer to assist him.

Dan closed the door behind him as the female deputy took her position against the wall. Laying his notebook on the table he took a seat across from the mysterious woman.

"Ma'am, I'm going to have to ask you to remove your glasses." Looking at her face, he pointed to the object of his request. There was a long pause before he saw her hesitantly raise her hand to her glasses. Hanging her head, she slowly removed them, keeping her eyes downcast as she did.

The sight that unfolded before him hit Dan like a ton of bricks. Behind the large framed glasses were black eyes and a nasty split above her cheekbone. "Ma'am, who did this to you?" Dan whispered feeling his rage boil to the surface.

"Um, um, I can't, um..."

"You have to tell me, ma'am," Dan persisted.

Whispering, "Um, my husband,"

Writing furiously on his notepad. "And his name?" Dan asked shaking his head in disgust.

"Really, sheriff, it really isn't that bad." Forcing a false smile to her battered face.

"His name, ma'am."

Whispering, dejectedly, "Matthew Monroe."

Dan dropped his pen at the name and ran his hands down his face. "Matthew Monroe is your husband?" Getting a slight nod, he went on, "And he did this to you?"

She gave another nod, before meekly adding, "It was a, um, misunderstanding and..."

"A misunderstanding? Ma'am you're lucky he didn't kill you." Pausing to get a better grip on the rage building inside him, he exhaled before speaking again. "Ma'am I think you should tell me everything."

CHAPTER EIGHTEEN

The door crashed open with the velocity of a bullet causing the dishes in the cupboards to rattle. Stephanie Monroe flew to her feet overturning the chair she had been seated in.

Through the opening came her husband, Matthew, with a look in his eye that made her blood turn to ice and her heart skip a beat. Plowing his way to her and gripping her arms tightly, she yelped in pain.

"WHAT DID YOU DO?"

Eyes wide with fear. "I…I…I…don't know what you mean, Matthew," she choked meekly.

"WHY IN THE HELL WOULD YOU CALL THE OLD LADIES HOUSE?" He spit, "HOW DARE YOU ISSUE AN ORDER TELLING ME TO GET HOME!" With that he shoved her away as if she thoroughly disgusted him. Falling to the floor, she scrambled to her knees begging, "I didn't call anyone, Matthew, I don't know what you're talkin' about, really I don't." Now sobbing hysterically.

"God, you are such a worthless bitch." Backhanding her, she landed across the room. Closing the gap between them, he grabbed her by the hair forcing her to look at him.

Her swollen eyes glistened with tears as they traveled the length of him to meet his. Stroking the side of her face with his free hand, his voice softened, "If I've told you once, I've told you a thousand times, the time I spend with her is off limits and of no concern to you."

Swallowing the sob in her throat. "But Matthew, she doesn't want you, when are you going to see that?"

The muscles he worked in his jaw relaxed when he flashed her a pearly smile before throwing his head back and laughing. "Doesn't want me? Ha, that's not quite the vibe I get from her." Adjusting his crotch, he turned away from the poor excuse of a woman on the floor.

Crawling on her knees, she grabbed his leg. "I wish you would look at me and want me the way you do her."

Chuckling louder he spat disgustedly, "You. You are nothing like her, look at you. You are nothing but a filthy cow and believe me baby, jealousy is not very becoming for you. What do you want? Huh? Do you want me to give you what I give her? Go ahead, tell me how bad you want it."

Suddenly the look in his eyes grew dark and menacing, she knew she had gone too far. Sauntering to her crumpled body, he slowly unzipped his jeans....

Swiping the tear from her cheek, Stephanie lowered her head in an attempt to hide her shame. "Um," sniffling she quietly said, "he then forced me to perform oral sex on him." Her hand was shaking as she tried to hide her face from Dan's pity filled eyes.

Speaking softly, "Take a breath, ma'am, I know..."

"Stephanie, um..., please call me Stephanie." Giving Dan a forlorn smile. "It makes me feel old when people call me ma'am."

Leaning forward, placing his arms on his notepad, Dan went on, "Okay then, Stephanie, I know this is very difficult, but I personally promise you Matthew Monroe will never get the opportunity to hurt you ever again." Pausing before he continued, "But I need you to help me make that happen. Can you do that?"

Taking a deep breath and releasing it, Stephanie Monroe slowly nodded her head.

Not realizing he was holding his own breath in anticipation, Dan exhaled. "Good," looking to the female deputy standing against the wall. "Can you get her some water?"

Once the deputy returned with the water, Stephanie gathered the courage to go on. Pushing a dull lock of brown hair behind her ear, she kept her eyes downcast as she cleared her throat. "After he was, um, finished..." she struggled for lack of a better word, "he, um, went to the fridge for a beer. He just stood there leaning against the fridge, smiling."

Dan studied the bruises on the battered woman's face, fuming inside. Men who did things like this to women he considered worse than animals. Careful not to press too hard. "What did you do then?"

Accepting the tissue the sheriff offered, Stephanie wiped at her nose. "Um, I didn't want to upset him again so I quietly stood up and went to the bedroom," sobbing again, "I felt so cheap, so dirty. I took a shower, and, um," wiping at her nose again, "I remember just standing in the shower, letting the water hit me and crying."

Stephanie Monroe was in her late twenties and even for a seasoned officer such as himself to see her like this—broken in every way—was heartbreaking.

"You're doing great, Stephanie. Just take your time."

Raising her eyes to the ceiling, Dan could see the shimmering pools of unfallen tears. "I just kept thinking, Why me? What have I done that was so terribly wrong for me to deserve this?"

Sobbing again, Dan let her cry a moment before patting her hand. "You didn't do anything to deserve this, no one deserves this. Your husband is an abuser and it's not your fault."

No one had ever told her that before, pulling herself together she went on, "After I had gone to bed, I could hear him on the phone with somebody."

"Do you know who?"

Shaking her head. "No I'm not sure, but it was probably his brother. He was speaking with such venom and hatred, it frightened me."

So the brother again! Great now there's two jackasses to deal with—Dan thought. "Could you hear what he was saying?"

At this point Stephanie lost control, laying her head on the table, she wept. "Um, oh my god, um, he was telling the person on the other end it was time to get rid of the two brats. That with them around he would never get her back."

Listening to the broken woman weep made Dan's heart break more. Hearing her last statement his eyes widened with shock. "WHAT?"

Eyes red and swollen from both the beating and the relentless crying, Stephanie for the first time looked directly into the sheriff's eyes, pleading, "Don't you see sheriff, I had to do it, I had to hide those two little girls because he was going to kill them," in a voice so low it was barely audible, "I'm sooo sorry."

CHAPTER NINETEEN

Dan left the station after giving strict orders to deputies to take Stephanie Monroe to the motel and stay with her. Fumbling with his keys, he made his way to his car and headed for the hospital.

He found Chase and Emily in the second floor waiting room. Acknowledging Emily's presence with a nod, Dan turned to Chase. "How are they?"

"Physically, Jenna's fine, the doctor wants to keep her overnight just to be on the safe side. He feels Laci will be here for awhile, because of her head injury. They've run some tests and there isn't any apparent damage to her brain, it's just watch and see."

"And mentally?" Dan questioned.

"Well he feels, through therapy they will learn to deal with the traumatizing events of the last few days."

Nodding sadly at the thought of the number of lives touched by the ordeal. "How's your mother handling all of this?"

"Hard, but she'll come through, we've sent her home to get some rest."

"I'm glad to hear it." Dan paused. "Um, Chase, that's not the only reason I'm here."

Curious, Chase searched Dan's face. "Oh?"

Motioning for Chase to take a seat as he pulled up a chair for himself. "Yeah, it's been quite a day." Shaking his head to get himself back on track. "Anyway, there has been a new development in the case."

Searching Dan's face and then looking at Emily. "New development? What do you mean, I thought it was over?"

"Well, I've recently learned, Laurel isn't the one after all who took the girls."

Thoroughly dumbstruck. "What? Dan, are you kidding me?" Chase was torn between relief it wasn't his sister and anger at the real culprit. "If not Laurel, then who?"

Dan released a sigh fearing Chase's reaction. "Stephanie Monroe."

His instincts were right on, Chase flew from his chair. "Stephanie Monroe? What the hell…"

Dan stood holding his hand against Chase's chest to keep him from doing something stupid. "Sit down, Chase, you need to hear me out before you go getting all riled up."

The younger man's eyes filled with contempt and fury as he searched the sheriff's face for answers. Emily rose from her chair and laid a gentle hand on Chase's back. "C'mon, sweetheart, let's hear what he has to say." She continued to rub her hand up and down. "Dan hasn't let us down so far, he at least should be allowed to explain."

Dan moved his eyes from Emily to Chase. Swallowing his anger, Chase nodded and eased himself back into his chair.

Emily and the sheriff returned to their seats. Having their full attention, Dan drew in a deep breath and began relating the story of Stephanie Monroe.

Having heard the full account of the miserable beating Stephanie Monroe endured and her attempt to save his nieces, Chase felt sheepish for his earlier outburst. He placed his hand over Emily's small one and gathered strength from it before whispering, sullenly, "Oh my god, I had no idea."

So many questions and thoughts were running rampant, Chase ran his fingers through his hair in an attempt to get them under control. Cradling his forehead in his hands, he quietly asked, "But how did she get in, and how did she take the girls without any of us knowing."

Watching the young couple struggle with their emotions, the pit in Dan's stomach grew. "Apparently, when Laurel and the girls were at your mother's house, Stephanie slipped in through the unlocked front door and hid in the empty spare bedroom."

Realizing the truth of the statement, Chase nodded. "Yes, we only lock the doors when we are away or go to bed. But I still don't understand how she did it."

"Tranquilizers. Before Laurel gave the girls a bath she poured them glasses of juice with the promise if they were good, they could have it. Stephanie Monroe slipped the tranquilizers into the glasses while Laurel was busy."

The thought of Laurel and the girls being drugged sent a cold chill up Chase's spine, he rose and walked to the window. He watched a woman walk her dog and followed her with his eyes until she turned the corner and disappeared from sight.

Slowly turning around. "I don't understand, how did she know about the storm cellar?"

"That was pure luck on her part, originally she was taking them to the barn. As she was walking in the pasture, she too stumbled on the rope."

Dan sat in silence, allowing Chase and Emily time to absorb the reality of the situation.

"What about Matthew and that jerk brother of his?" Chase asked dripping with venom.

"Deputies are, as we speak, bringing them in. Believe me it will be a long time before they will be able to do this to anyone again."

EPILOGUE

Six months later perched on the fence surrounding the pasture, Chase and Emily watched as the girls fed the horses.

Sifting their fingers through the bucket of oats, Jenna and Laci watched as it fell into little piles. Giggling and squealing they dropped their bucket and ran as a little mouse hiding in the oats jumped at them.

Laughing at the sight, Emily commented as she snuggled closer to Chase's side. "You almost could never tell they were in such a traumatizing ordeal,"

Looking at the fading blotch on Laci's forehead, sadness clouded his eyes. "Mmm, their nightmares are getting fewer and farther between. They will heal, they are strong girls."

Emily laid her head against his arm. "I wish we could say the same for Laurel."

Lowering his eyes to the ground, Chase nodded his head. Laurel's condition was no better today than that day six months ago. His heart broke every time he thought of her in the psychiatric hospital with the inability to distinguish between what is and isn't real. A judge had awarded him guardianship of the girls, after determining the extent of Matthew's resentment and abuse towards Jenna and his mother was just not able to care for them because of her age.

Stepping down from the fence, Chase grasped Emily around the waist and helped her to the ground. Entering the barn, he returned with a blanket and spread it at her feet. Taking a more comfortable seat on the blanket, they focused again on the girls.

Glancing down into Emily's beautiful brown eyes. "So are you ready to marry me and take on a ready-made family, Emily Plackart?" Chase paused and then added, "I can't guarantee our life will be easy, because I am learning as I go, but I can guarantee you how much I love you."

Her heart melted at the sight of his dazzling dimples. "Of course, I will marry you, I love you with all my heart and while we provide the girls with a loving two parent home, we may be adding another little one..."

Chase searched Emily's face as she smiled up at him. "Emily are you saying you're..."

Nodding she threw her arms around his neck as he captured her lips with his. Emily and Chase broke apart laughing, as the girls once again spotted the mouse and bounded on to their laps.

"Happy?" She asked over the top of Laci's head.

"More than I ever knew possible." Gathering all three of his girls into his arms in a big bear hug, his lips found hers over the giggling heads of the precious little girls lost.